Mark Wilson – for my brother Leigh,
his love of the sea
and his beautiful wooden boats.

Many thanks to Leonie Scanlan for her help and research during this project.

James Cook's Endeavour Journal was the main source for my research. It is in the collection of the National Library of Australia.

I have used the term 'Great South Land' throughout for readability, except in the quote from James Cook's 'secret orders' on page 12.

Wherever possible, I have endeavoured to respectfully use clan group names for the First Nations people referred to in this narrative. However, the term 'natives' is used in Isaac Smith's journal entries to be consistent with its common use in the late 1700s. It is also the term used in quotes I have taken from Cook's own journal, and also his written orders from the British Admiralty.

First published in 2021 by Windy Hollow Books
PO Box 265, Kew East, Victoria, Australia 3102
www.windyhollowbooks.com.au
www.facebook.com/windyhollowbooks

ISBN: 9781922081858 (hardback)

Design by Nuovo Group

A catalogue record for this book is available from the National Library of Australia

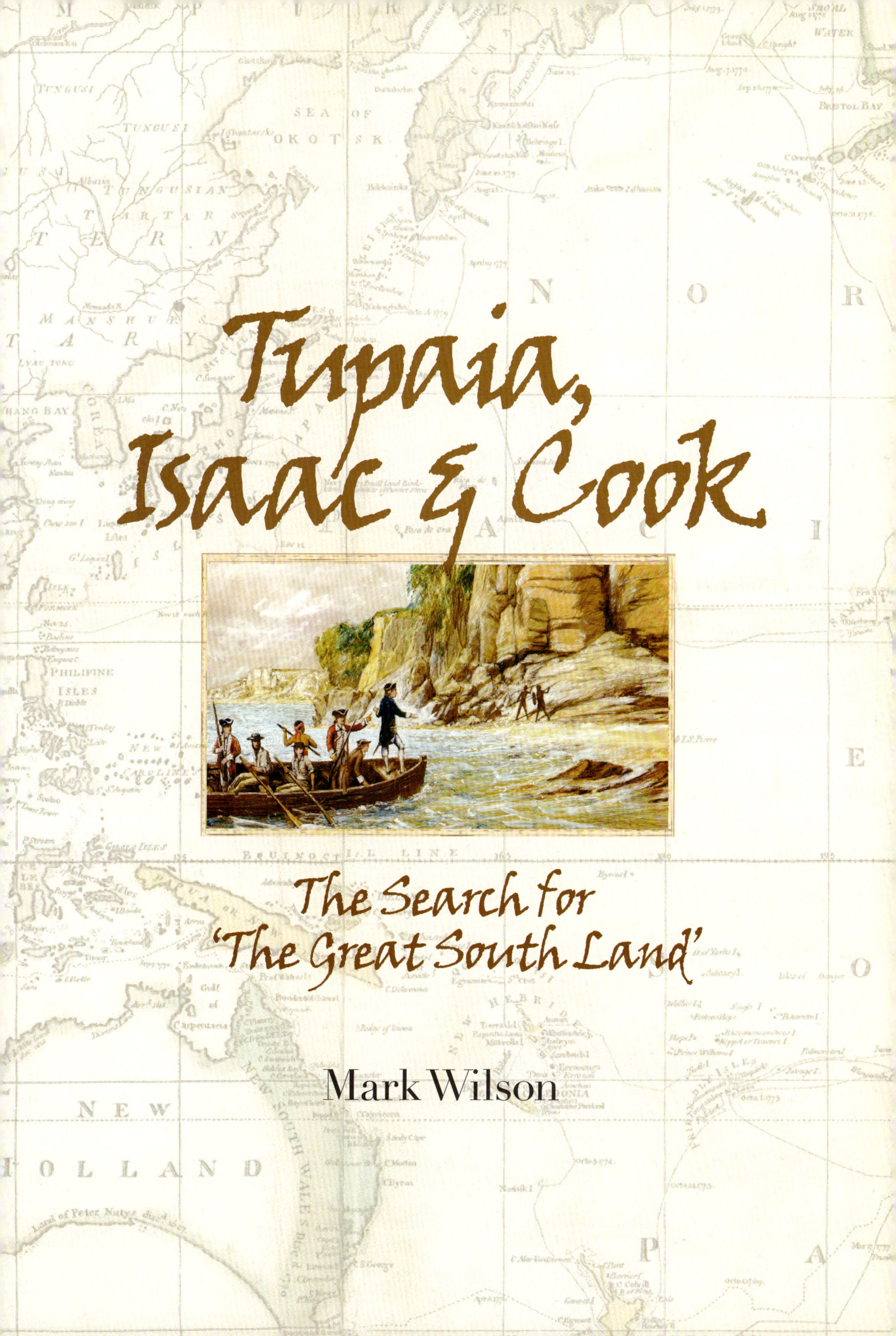
Tupaia, Isaac & Cook
The Search for 'The Great South Land'
Mark Wilson

Introduction

The year was 1769 and a young Rai'aitean master navigator named Tupaia boarded the ship Endeavour. It was in Tahitian waters and on board was a young sailor named Isaac Smith, who was a cousin of the captain's wife.

We follow the epic voyage of the Endeavour as the story unfolds through the pages of Isaac's personal diary. Also on board is Joseph Banks, a wealthy naturalist, and James Cook, the captain of the Endeavour.

The journey the four men undertook together changed the course of history and altered forever the lives of many people throughout the Pacific.

The eldest of seven children, Isaac was just 13 when he joined the Royal Navy as an able seaman. His cousin Elizabeth had married Lieutenant James Cook, a captain in the Royal Navy, and Isaac was assigned to James Cook's ship, the Grenville.

His first voyage was to Newfoundland, and in the evenings in the captain's cabin, James taught Isaac how to plot and draw maps of the coastline.

Thousands of miles away, on a small island in the middle of the Pacific Ocean, a boy listens to his father as he tells stories about the stars, sun, moon and tides, and how — if he follows the sea birds on their migration, like his ancestors, he will be able to find his way across the ocean. The boy's name is Tupaia.

When Isaac returned to England from Newfoundland, James Cook announced that he was going on a long voyage, and the wealthy scientist Joseph Banks would be sailing with him. This new voyage sounded mysterious and exciting, so Isaac said farewell to his family before hurrying down to the docks.

At that moment, off a coral reef just south of the Marquesas Islands, a Tahitian war canoe is driving through the ocean. Tupaia is in front of his father, who calls to 'paddle hard'. Tupaia's arms ache, but he has to keep paddling, for this is part of his training, to become a man and understand the ways of the sea.

There is a strange ship in the bay when they return home. It's called the Dolphin, and Tupaia goes aboard to meet the captain. His name is Wallis, and over the next few weeks, the captain teaches Tupaia to speak English.

Isaac was the first crew member to board the refitted coal carrier with a brand new name — HMB Endeavour. He made notes in his diary after he finished his duties for the day.

August 24, 1768, Plymouth. England.

James is an excellent sea captain and a very good mapmaker, even though he is only a lieutenant. He seldom raises his voice and all the men like him.

We have loaded the ship with food, livestock, and tools for building, mining and gardening. Mr. Banks and his assistants brought strange equipment aboard and stowed it all carefully in the captain's cabin. There are whispers among the crew that the captain has secret orders to find a strange new land, full of silks and spices, silver and gold. If it's true, we will all be rich!

Tupaia becomes a man this day, and celebrates by receiving ancient marks on his body. He now calls to the gods to keep his family safe, for he must leave them and undertake his first journey alone across the ocean.

On August 25, 1768, the Endeavour left Plymouth Harbour, then sailed south into the Atlantic Ocean. Isaac loved life at sea. The work was hard and sometimes dangerous, but also exciting.

The first stop was Madeira and then Rio de Janeiro, where they took on fresh water and supplies. Isaac loved the warmth and the people there.

Far away, Tupaia sets sail, alone in the vastness of the great ocean. Using all the skills and knowledge his father has taught him, Tupaia follows the stars, wind and tides. For the first seven days, he doesn't paddle, simply letting his hand drift in the water by the side of the boat so he can feel the current, letting it take him on his journey.

The Endeavour sailed on, passing the Falkland Islands, where Isaac saw penguins for the first time, but when they arrived at Tierra del Fuego, tragedy struck.

While ashore collecting plant specimens, two of the party, Dorlton and Richmond, fell ill after being caught in a snow storm. They both passed away during the night.

Back on board, some of the crew saw this as a bad omen, but the Endeavour set sail again and rounded Cape Horn, South America. Isaac was up in the rigging, hanging on for dear life, while the ship plunged through waves almost as tall as the main mast.

Many miles away, Tupaia is also caught in a storm. His little boat is tossed around from wave to wave, so Tupaia lies in the bottom of the boat and waits for the storm to pass. When it does, he goes fishing on a nearby island, then looks up to the night sky at the stars. They will guide him home.

On June 3, 1769, it was a fine day as Tupaia paddled home.
Rounding the headland of Matavia Bay, Tahiti, he was surprised to see a big ship like the Dolphin he had seen as a boy.
As Tupaia paddled past he saw a boy watching him and waved.
He found out later, the boy's name was Isaac.

Aboard the Endeavour, the captain announced that in a few days they were going to observe the transit of Venus across the sun.
He told the crew: *'I want every man present to endeavor, by every fair means, to cultivate a friendship with the Natives and to treat them with all imaginable humanity'.*

July 12, 1769, Tahiti.

These past few months have been so exciting. We met the Chiefs and explored other islands with the captain, Mr. Banks and Tupaia, a young Tahitian and his assistant Tiata. They will be sailing with us when we leave Tahiti, and the captain says Tupaia is a very good interpreter and navigator.

Tupaia has drawn a map for the captain, which shows all the islands for miles around. He says he hasn't visited all of them, but simply knows where they are by the stars. He is also a very good artist. We swapped drawings and he laughed when he saw my drawing of him!

On the eve of their departure from Tahiti, the captain made an announcement to the officers. Isaac was with Tupaia in the chart room nearby, and overheard them talking. The captain said he had secret orders to search for the 'Great Southern Continent'. He then said:

'In the event that we find the Great Southern Continent, and with the consent of the natives, we are to take possession of convenient situations in the country in the name of the King of Great Britain'.

Isaac wondered what the people living in the Great South Land would be like, and if he would be welcomed there.

The Endeavour sailed from Tahiti on July 13, and the search for the mysterious 'Great South Land' began.

After weeks of searching to the south and finding only a few small islands, the Endeavour sailed west. The weather soon closed in and the ship was lashed by storms of sheeting rain and hail. Then one blustery morning early in October, Tupaia pointed at some sea birds flying westward. 'Those birds don't go far from land,' he said. 'So we will see land soon', he added with a smile. Sure enough, just before nightfall, the crew saw mountains in the distance.

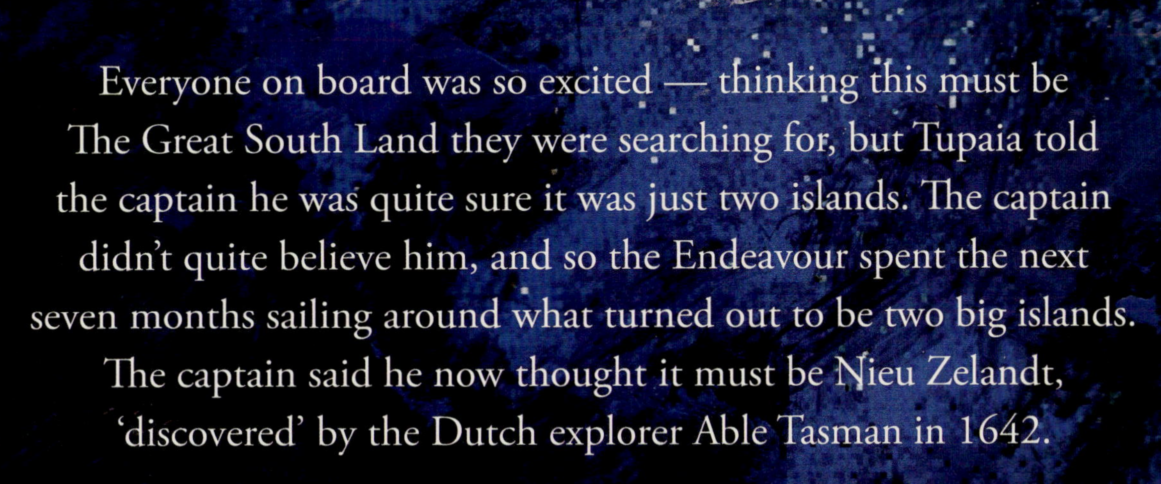

Everyone on board was so excited — thinking this must be The Great South Land they were searching for, but Tupaia told the captain he was quite sure it was just two islands. The captain didn't quite believe him, and so the Endeavour spent the next seven months sailing around what turned out to be two big islands. The captain said he now thought it must be Nieu Zelandt, 'discovered' by the Dutch explorer Able Tasman in 1642.

April 3, 1770, Pacific Ocean.

Our meetings with the natives here didn't go well. They were friendly at first, then there were clashes. When we beached the Endeavour for cleaning, the natives did a war dance and looked angry and threatening, and shots were fired. On another day, over a hundred natives in nine big war canoes attacked our ship. Three of the natives were killed in the battle. Eventually, Tupaia approached their warriors and talked to them in his own language, and they finally settled down. We were lucky to have him on board.

Mr. Banks and his assistant collected wild celery before we left. We mix it with oatmeal for breakfast. Mr. Banks says it will stop us getting the disease called Scurvy.

The captain called a meeting on the day of departure. He said that so far, he had failed to find the 'Great South Land', and he asked the officers: 'Do we turn back the way we have come, and give up our search, or do we continue west into unknown and uncharted waters?'

It was agreed to continue westward, and so they did. At night, Tupaia and Isaac did drawings of all they had seen. But then fierce storms raced in from the south west, blowing the ship off course as it plunged through enormous swells. The sea became increasingly rough as sheets of rain lashed the Endeavour, and many aboard began to fear what might lay ahead.

It was dawn, April 19, 1770 when land was sighted. The Endeavour turned northeast with a gentle breeze, following the coast for several days, then entered a shallow bay. The captain took Isaac, Tupaia and Mr. Banks towards the shore, where two men of the Gweagal clan stood watching them. The captain threw trinkets from the boat onto the beach as gifts, but the two warriors were not distracted by this and raised their spears.

The captain waited for a short time, wondering what he could do. Then he raised his musket and fired a warning shot near them. In reply, the older of the two warriors threw a rock at the captain, which just missed his head. The captain fired back, wounding the warrior.

April 30, 1770, East Coast of New Holland.

When the boat finally pulled up onto the sand, the wounded native and his friend had disappeared. The captain said to me, 'Jump out Isaac'. It was a huge honor to be the first one ashore, and one I will never forget. While we were there, we explored the land around the bay. I had never seen anything like it! There were strange animals, insects and plants, which Mr. Banks was very excited about. There were lots of brightly coloured birds in the trees and huge stingrays in the water.

Heading north again, there was a strange feeling of foreboding amongst the crew as the Endeavour passed a long sandy island. A Butchulla man on the beach waved at the ship and pointed ahead. Then others joined him and did the same. The captain thought they were being threatening, but Tupaia thought they were pointing ahead, perhaps trying to warn of danger there.

The Endeavour sailed on…
into a massive tangle of dangerous reefs.

The captain used all his skills to thread the Endeavour between the shore and the submerged reefs as they continued northwards. The night closed in, and they pressed on into the darkness.

But something was wrong. It was close to midnight. Isaac and Tupaia couldn't sleep and were up on deck. Isaac went to the railing, and froze in shock! In the lantern light he could see something dark and silent, looming up beside the ship. He tried to call out, but just as he did…

Bang! It was like an explosion — a massive piece of coral punched through the wooden hull of the ship, sending men sprawling onto the deck. The Endeavor was stranded on a coral reef. The captain stayed calm and began issuing orders. 'Start the pumps!' he shouted, as gallons of water poured through the jagged hole in the hull. 'We also need to lighten the ship,' he said.

So Tupaia and Isaac helped drag some of the cannons to the side and hurl them into the water. But none of this helped float the ship off the reef, so the captain ordered the anchor be rowed out and dropped over the edge of the reef. They would use it to 'pull' the ship off the reef when the tide was high.

Every man aboard took turns on the capstan wheel and the pumps, even Mr. Banks — heaving until their muscles ached and they fell to the deck exhausted. Tupaia and Isaac took their turns as well.

Almost 24 hours after they hit the reef, Isaac and Tupaia were pushing hard on the wheel, when the ship began to move — each wave lifted the ship a little higher. They all pushed even harder now and suddenly the Endeavour floated free!

A great cheer went up from the crew, but they weren't out of danger yet. They would need to seal the hole in the hull quickly, as the pumps couldn't keep the water out.
The captain ordered Isaac and the other crewmen to drag a canvas sail right under the ship until it covered the hole.
Called 'fothering', it was like a giant bandage, with a sticky mixture of wool, rope, oakum and manure to seal the hole.

For five days, the Endeavour carefully sailed for the mainland, and was soon safely beached at a place the captain named Endeavour River. The crew set about repairing the hull, but after looking around, Tupaia thought the beach might be a 'sacred' place, so perhaps they shouldn't be there.

It was four weeks later when men of the Guugu Yimithirr people finally came to see the 'strangers'. They sat with Tupaia on the beach and came back again during the following week.

The captain was pleased that they had finally met and made peace. It was only a week later, however, when a Guugu Yimithirr warrior became angry after seeing turtles the crew had caught; as turtles were considered sacred to his people. The warrior set fire to the crew's camp. So the captain fired a musket, wounding the warrior who then ran off.

August 22, 1770, Possession Island.

We soon set sail again but still had to find our way through the dangerous reefs, with every single person on board looking out for the jagged rocks and coral. We were almost swept onto the reef twice by the currents — we were so close! It was a lucky escape, but we eventually cleared the reefs and arrived at Possession Island, named by the captain when we went ashore.

The British flag was raised and the captain made a speech, in which he claimed all the land along the coast in the name of King George the Third. Some native people came to watch us, and I wondered if they knew what it all meant. Did these people even want to be ruled by our King George, who was living on the other side of the world?

Tupaia is very sick now. The captain thinks he has scurvy…

October 26, 1770, Batavia.

Whatever happens, I will be forever proud to say that Tupaia was my friend, and we sailed with James Cook and Mr. Banks. The captain has taught me how to be a good sailor and mapmaker, and Tupaia has taught me about the stars, tides, and the ways of his people. We arrived in Batavia on October 11, but there were no celebrations. Many of the crew have fallen victim to disease, some have died, and now Tupaia's illness is getting worse.

November 19, 1770, Batavia.

I write this entry in my diary with a heavy heart. I sat with Tupaia all through the night, and it broke my heart to see my strong, proud friend, so pale and weak from fever. We sat together on the deck of the Endeavour and I held him, because he couldn't sit up. He asked me to help him turn towards the east, the direction of his home. Then he squeezed my hand and whispered, 'Isaac, you are my friend. We have journeyed far together with our captain and Mr. Banks, and we have had many adventures, but now I must leave you, as the spirits beckon me home…'

Afterword

The Endeavour finally arrived back in England on 13th July, 1771. The 'discovery' of places like Tahiti, Australia and New Zealand were only discoveries for Europeans — places where people have been living for thousands of years with their own identity, culture and traditions. We also know that these 'discoveries' paved the way for many injustices towards the First Nation peoples. We can't change history, but we can learn from it — and hopefully move towards the future with an understanding and compassion for all people.

James Cook was under secret orders by the Admiralty in England to find 'The Great South Land' and claim it for Britain. In this he succeeded. My extensive research for this book shows he displayed compassion for his crew and others he met — also bravery, determination and patience, all of which eventually made him one of the greatest sea captains, navigators and explorers in history. The charts and maps he made, some with the help of the great Rai'aitean navigator Tupaia and others, were so accurate they can still be followed today. That he made most of them from the deck of the dipping and swaying Endeavour, is truly remarkable.

Tupaia was also one of the greatest navigators of all time. His instruments were the sun, moon, wind, stars, tides, and the migratory paths of sea birds. He also had the wisdom passed down by many generations of ancestral seafarers. His knowledge was invaluable to James Cook and his explorations. Tupaia never recovered from his illness while the Endeavour was in Batavia; his dream to go to England to meet King George the Third was never realised. Tupaia died of typhoid shortly before Christmas, 1770, many thousands of miles from his beloved Rai'aitean island home. His assistant Tiata, grief stricken at the passing of his master, died soon after. Across the islands of the Pacific, Tupaia's epic journey aboard the Endeavour is still spoken of with reverence today.

Isaac Smith became the first 'European' to set foot on eastern Australian soil – James Cook telling him, 'Jump out, Isaac', as the ship's boat touched the shore at Stingray Bay, now called Botany Bay. Isaac was the cousin of Elizabeth Cook, the wife of Captain James Cook, and after the famous voyage, stayed in the Royal Navy until he retired. He was Elizabeth's constant companion after James Cook was tragically killed in Hawaii on February 14, 1779. In his Will, Isaac left all his wealth to the poor.

James Cook's copy of Tupaia's map of the Pacific islands. C. 1769. Though Tupaia had never visited many of the islands, Cook said Tupaia's map was incredibly accurate.